ADVENTURE HOLIDAY

by Cheryl Brown

B⬡XTREE

First published in the UK 1993 by BOXTREE LTD, Broadwall House, 21 Broadwall,
London SE1 9PL
1 3 5 7 9 10 8 6 4 2
Copyright © 1993 ITC ENTERTAINMENT GROUP LTD.
Licensed by Copyright Promotions Ltd.
Design and illustrations by Arkadia
1-85283-577 x

Printed in Scotland by Cambus Litho Ltd.

A catalogue record for this book is available from the British Library

This is Melody Angel. Melody is a pilot. She flies a jet plane.

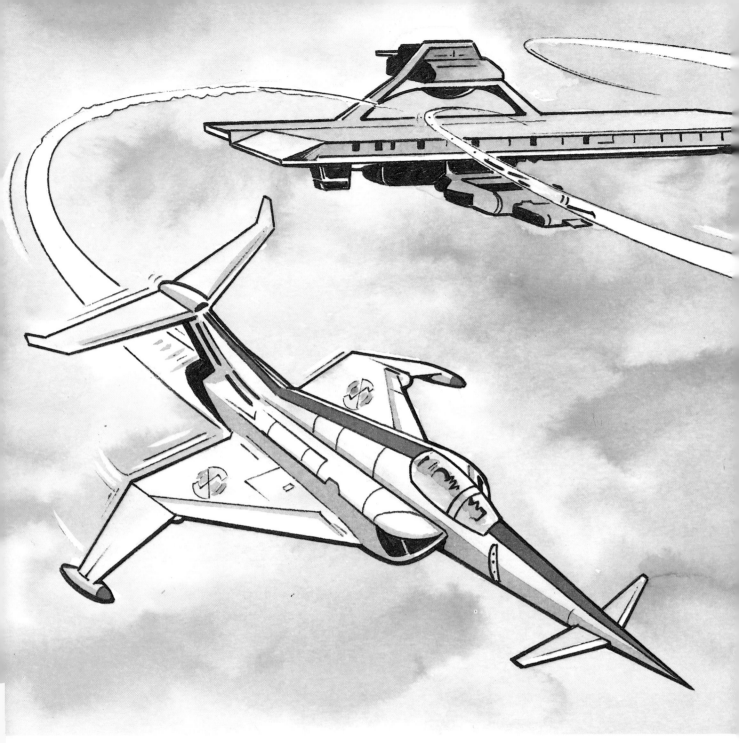

Melody and her friends - Rhapsody, Harmony, Symphony and Destiny - live and work on Cloudbase, the headquarters of Spectrum, the World Security Agency.

The Angels are always ready for action.

Today Melody is going on holiday. She says goodbye to her friends and climbs on board a Spectrum helicopter. Captain Grey will take her back down to land to collect her car.

'Have a good time,' her friends say as they wave goodbye to her.
'I will,' says Melody.

Captain Grey lands the helicopter in the car park. He helps Melody put her bag in the boot of the car. They are so busy they do not notice a man dressed in black creeping away.

Soon the car is packed. 'Send me a postcard,' says Captain Grey as he waves goodbye to Melody.

Back on Cloudbase, Colonel White has had a message from the Mysterons. No one knows what the Mysterons look like, but they are always up to no good. The Mysterons' message says that

Melody's holiday will be even more eventful than she had planned.
'What can it mean?' asks Lieutenant Green.
'Only one thing,' says Colonel White. 'Trouble!'

Melody is driving her car down a long winding hill. She puts her foot on the brake to slow the car down. The brakes do not work. Someone has tampered with them.

She uses her radio to call for help. 'Come in, Cloudbase,' she says, 'I'm in trouble!'

'This is the work of the Mysterons and their agent Captain Black,' says Colonel White. 'Don't worry, Melody, we will send our best man to help you.'

Colonel White contacts Captain Scarlet. Captain Scarlet is on patrol with Captain Blue and Captain Magenta. 'We're on our way,' he says.

Captain Blue flies the Spectrum helicopter as quickly as he can. 'I just hope we reach her in time,' he says.

'We will,' says Captain Scarlet. 'Look. There she is.'
They can see Melody's car on the road below, speeding out of control.

The helicopter flies above the speeding car.
'Hang on, Melody,' shouts Captain Scarlet.

Captain Magenta lowers Captain Scarlet into the car on the end of a rope. He drops into the seat next to Melody.

Captain Scarlet clips a hook onto Melody's belt. The hook is attached to a rope. Captain Scarlet pulls on the rope.

This is the signal for Captain Magenta to winch Melody up into the helicopter. He pulls her to safety.

Suddenly Captain Scarlet sees a herd of cattle in the road ahead. He swerves to miss them and speeds into the farmyard.

He splashes through the duckpond and crashes into the barn doors.

Captain Blue lands the helicopter and Melody runs across the farmyard. Captain Scarlet staggers out of the barn.

'Are you hurt?' asks Melody.

'No, you know I'm indestructible,' says Captain Scarlet, 'but I'm very glad you only have one holiday a year!'